VICTORIAN
STORIES
OF EXETER

for
Richard and Meg

CHRISTMAS IN DEVON

VICTORIAN
STORIES
OF EXETER

T O D D   G R A Y

First published in Great Britain by The Mint Press, 2001

ISBN 1–903356–18–0

Cataloguing in Publication Data
CIP record for this title is available from the British Library

The Mint Press
18 The Mint
Exeter, Devon
England EX4 3BL

Text and cover design by Delphine Jones

Printed and bound in Great Britain
by Short Run Press Ltd, Exeter.

CONTENTS

INTRODUCTION

It was a common practice in the late nineteenth century for newspapers to serialise short stories. Nearly all were taken from national publications but one Devon paper carried locally written and set fiction in one issue in the year: the last newspaper before Christmas carried special Christmas stories. Most of these featured the festive season and were generally good-natured and convivial in tone. All three of the stories in this collection appeared in Christmas issues of *The Devon Weekly Times*; 'Hidden Treasures of Exeter Cathedral' by Frederick Thomas was published on 26 December 1890, 'Through the North Gate: A Story of Christmas Eve' by 'Iris' on 24 December 1897 and 'Miss Jefferson's Baby: A Story of Christmas Eve, 1781' by Frederick Thomas on 23 December 1881.

It is most likely that these stories were specially commissioned by the newspaper. Little however is known about the writers. 'Iris' wrote other short stories for local newspapers in the 1890s but it has not been possible to identify her: one other woman who also wrote local short stories was Beatrice Cresswell.   In 1882 Frederick Thomas published *Humours and other poetic pictures: legends and stories of Devon* and may have been the Hatter of that name who had business premises on the High Street in Exeter.

Both writers are concerned with topographical features which would have been familiar to their readers but the writers demonstrated a less reliable understanding of local history.   The first story in particular combines historical fact with a great deal of imagination.   Even some of the place names are misleading: one character refers to 'Allhallows Green' a hundred years before it could have been given that name.   But these stories were not meant to be serious: they were offered as enjoyment for the festive season.

Hidden Treasures of Exeter Cathedral

FREDERICK THOMAS

1890

How seldom, when passing through the old Cathedral Yard – which, notwithstanding its many transformations for 'better and for worse' still retains sufficient of its historic character to carry us back to past ages – do we think of those changing scenes and troublous times upon which the grand old structure has looked down during the past six hundred years.

The strange and grotesque surroundings of the Cathedral tell the tale of many changes in architectural ideas. There is the quaint example of ancient style; the grand modern bank; the ecclesiastical looking business warehouse; the comfortable modern hotel; the old inn; the snug dwelling-house; the modest little shop; and, standing out like a painful intrusion, is a sort of petrified façade of Barnum's Museum with fossilised 'variegated lamps' round the tasteless windows.

Yet, despite modern innovations, some of them sadly out of place and out of taste, there still remains to keep the venerable pile company, enough to arrest the mind of the student and enable him, as it were, to live and move amongst the times and scenes of his ancestors.

There stands the grand old Cathedral itself, frowning and stately as when some poor wretch paid with his or her tribute to ignorance, bigotry and superstition, on that spot where each Fifth of November the huge bonfire sends its many tongues of flame to illume the western sky.

But to our story.

When 'Bluff King Hal', as some historians have named that unscrupulous and much-married monarch, had been enabled, by the subtle reasoning of the virtuous and saintly Cranmer, to set aside his vows to his wife and his oath to the Constitution, and was – with the aid of his courtly sycophants – concocting the most colourable excuse for plundering all the ecclesiastical and monastic institutions of the land, it was represented to his Majesty that Devonshire was by far the fattest of them all, and that the See of Exeter boasted the wealthiest abbeys and monasteries.

So it was intended that this wholesale

'confiscation' should be kept a profound secret until the most opportune moment to carry out the 'work'.

But there was one in that Secret Council who was determined, though at a general risk, to inform the Bishop of Exon of the design of his Diocese. This was Roderick Vanstone, son of the Baron of Shillingford, and one of Henry's spiritual attendants. He had taken his vows at Cowick Abbey; and was, by the influence of the Abbot of Polsloe, attached to the Court. Although dutiful to his King, he was faithful to his Creed.

So by the aid of a trustworthy servant, whom he sent professedly on a domestic mission to Devon, the Bishops, Priests and Abbots were forewarned.

It was then the Bishop and his faithful clergy put their heads together, and gathering all the most precious and valuable property contained in the Churches, Abbeys and Monasteries of the Diocese, deposited them in a secret vault beneath the South Tower of the Cathedral, and known only to the Bishop, and the three Priors of St Nicholas, Kenn and Cowick.

At this time there existed four secret passages to the Cathedral, known only by successional oath to the heads of the three establishments. And, fortunately, the Governor of Rougemont Castle, being a fresh importation, and not an ecclesiastic, was unaware of any communication from the Watch Tower, which still exists in the Rougemont Grounds. When the blow came and the plunder began, they found that no Diocese was so poor in convertible wealth as that of Devon.

The treasure deposited in this secret

vault was of enormous value, and was now in the custody of the 'sworn' four.

But the wily emissaries of Henry suspected, from the almost too barren condition of the establishments and the altars, that treasure had been hidden, and by dint of bribery, persecution, and cruelty they learned that there were subterranean passages in different parts of the city. But they could not discover their whereabouts, or whence or where these passages led, and little they dreamed that they all converged under old St Peter's towers. The approach to the vaults from Rougemont had been blocked by solid masonry in the subterranean passage by men brought blind-fold from Kirton and taken back in the same way.

Their work was completed not a moment too soon. The effigy and large tomb which concealed the blocked entrance had been removed from another part of the Cathedral to this recess, and looked old and undisturbed.

It was a grand and solemn sight when, in forced compliance with Henry's decree, the Bishop, priests, fathers, altar boys and robed attendants moved down the centre aisle of the grand old building, to the strains of Ave Maria on the great organ, and out into the open green. Tears dimmed the eyes of the faithful, and lamentations were heard all around, whilst at the South entrance there filed in the newly-accredited ecclesiastics, who had preferred to accept the sovereignty of the King to that of the Pope.

No sooner had this change in the authority taken place, than petty persecution against the Roman Catholic institutions began; and the belief that they had hidden the wealth so greatly coveted, gave an excuse for tormenting the fallen Brotherhoods in divers ways.

Two of the four who held the secret of the hidden treasure had been hanged for refusing to disclose; and one evening an officer, with six armed soldiers, appeared at the house of the Vicar of St Thomas, and with insolent bearing addressed him thus:

'There is ample information, that thou hast all along been cognisant of the whereabouts of the stolen property of His Majesty the King.'

With flashing eyes the Vicar replied:

'I know not of what you speak.'

'Then', said the officer, taking a sealed letter from his belt and placing it on the table, 'we will be here at sundown tomorrow, and if the information required of thee be not then forthcoming, thou mayst break that seal and read its contents.'

Next day the officer appeared with a larger number of soldiers. The Vicar again protested that he knew nothing of what he demanded.

'Then open the packet,' said the officer in command.

The vicar did so, and read therein of his own death warrant, and in spite of his protestations, he was drawn up to the top of the Tower, and for several days and nights the lifeless body of the good old man swung to and fro in the wind.

The rage of the baffled despoilers of the altars knew no bounds, and the last diabolical act, which cut off all chances of Henry recovering the hidden treasure, was soon afterwards perpetrated.

It was New Year's Eve. There was a gentle fall of snow, which hung like a winding sheet about the old city and surroundings. The monks of St Nicholas, although deposed, were seeing 'the old year out and the new year in' with their wonted admixture of devotion and merry-making, as the bell of St Peter boomed forth the midnight hour, and Brother Rupert had scarcely raised his horn, and amid a fervent 'Amen' had proposed 'To our speedy restoration' when a loud knocking at the Bartholomew Gate of the Priory startled the holy fathers, and, as they crossed themselves, Prior Renfrew appeared looking ghastly pale.

'Fathers,' he began, 'there is some trouble for us, as I see from my chamber fifty or sixty soldiers of the King.'

'We fear them not,' said Brother Samuel; 'bid them explain their presence here this New Year's morn.'

But before another word could be spoken, the captain of the troop rushed into the apartment, and looking contemptuously upon the well-filled board, exclaimed, 'Little wonder that the poor Fathers of St Nicholas can live on the fat of the land whilst they have the wealth of the country from which to replenish their larders.'

Then, turning to Renfrew and Brother Silas, he hissed, rather than spoke 'For nearly two years have ye defied and baffled the will of our beloved King. But your set have paid with their lives for the stubbornness of their hearts. We have now learned that you (pointing to Renfrew and Silas), you only, know the whereabouts of the plunder.'

'Plunder!' rejoined Brother Adrian, his large blue eyes flashing, 'we are no plunderers; if thou want'st plunder, this Priory is no place to seek it.'

'I want no banter,' retorted the officer,

'The presence of these two is required at Rougemont Castle at once.'

'Most willingly,' simultaneously replied Renfrew and Silas; and, without further ceremony, the two venerable Fathers were marching, surrounded by soldiers, through Allhallows Green, up St David's Valley, to the back entrance to Rougemont Castle.

Here they were at once confronted with the Governor of the Castle, who addressed them thus: 'Far be it from us to adopt the means with which our beloved King hath invested us, but his dogged and unseeming defiance of his Majesty's will and pleasure must, and shall, most speedily meet its just reward. We have obtained, no matter how, reliable information that you, and you only, know the spot where lies hidden the property of his most sacred Majesty.'

'We know of no property belonging to the King!' sharply retorted Father Silas. But the governor waived his hand, and proceeded:

'It is decreed that with three trusty officers you proceed and make known the way to the whereabouts of the treasure. This done, we are empowered to pardon all those who aided in the retention of the King's rightful property; but, should you still decline this proferred clemency, then, within twelve hours from this time, your carcasses will hang in the Castle-yard.'

The two priests, pale and resolute, looked at each other, and, almost as with one voice, exclaimed, 'We have nothing to communicate.'

The brow of the Governor darkened, and, turning to his lieutenant, remarked, 'We will give them four hours, and then you know your instructions.' The officer bowed, beckoned the priests, and conducted them to a small apartment overlooking the Long brook. Here he locked them in, and set a guard on the door.

As soon as they felt they were alone, 'Merciful heavens!' ejaculated Renfrew. 'I have the ground plans and key on my person. How can we convey them to our Brethren, for there are but two courses open to us, death or revelation – what shall it be?'

Silas, as his eyes glistened with moisture, calmly responded, 'It must not be revelation'. They clasped each other's hand, and with a seeming disregard of the fate that awaited them, calmly discussed how and by what means the plan and key could be conveyed to St Nicholas Priory. One chance only seemed possible to them.

The door was opened, and the officer asked, 'Are you prepared to comply with the wishes of the Governor?'

'We desire to speak with his Excellency. Pray conduct us to him.'

'I will go to him with you message,' said the officer. And leaving soldiers in charge, proceeded to the Governor, who came back with the officer, and enquired their will.

'We desire,' began Silas, 'to be allowed to confer with our Brethren of St Nicholas, that we may draw up a prayer to His Majesty that no such step as that now contemplated be taken.'

The Governor smiled, and shook his head, 'My instructions are definite, and this cannot be granted.'

'Then,' said Father Renfrew, 'allow us to see one of our brothers that we may send our last words of affection to them.'

Again he shook his head, and said, 'You and your Brethren have fooled us too long, and unless you are prepared at once to disclose, you must prepare to meet your punishment.'

The doomed priests exchanged glances, and Silas made the last and only remaining effort to convey the plans and key of St Nicholas Priory.

Appealing to the Governor he rejoined, 'You surely would not subject our bodies to any indignity. May we ask that they may be handed over to our own people and taken for burial to the Priory and that our brethren only shall perform these last offices.'

'This much I grant you,' resumed the Governor, 'but you are surely not such blind dolts as to prefer death to duty.'

'We have nothing to communicate,' was the calm and dignified response.

'Then, by my faith, the last prayer you will ever utter had better be said quickly.'

The snow had ceased to fall and the pale moon shone on the glistening particles and also upon two dark shadowy forms suspended beneath one of the stately trees in the Castle Yard. But the hope that when their bodies were handed over to their brethren of St Nicholas, the plan and key would be recovered, was vain.

It so happened that when the two soldiers who had instructions to cut down and deliver up the dead Fathers were performing the task, one of them felt, inside the frock of Brother Renfrew, what proved to be the ground plan and key, and having become acquainted with the subject of the hidden treasure, they suspected enough of the truth to cause them to hide their find without saying a word to their officers. When the bodies were delivered to the sorrowing Brotherhood, there was nothing to indicate that either had a secret to impart. But the plan, key, and hurriedly-written notes of explanation the soldiers had appropriated, although they would have been intelligible at the Priory, proved but a fatal legacy to their possessors.

That evening, when off duty, the two soldiers examined the notes and plan, which clearly indicated the locality of the Castle entrance to the subterranean way, and watching their opportunity, carefully examined the floor of the Watch Tower. By removing some large stones they found the opening. These they replaced, and, taking advantage of leave of absence, provided themselves with flint and steel, torches, and some candles, and managed unobserved to enter the thicket at the base of the tower still existing in the grounds of Rougemont. They again removed the stones to make an aperture sufficiently large to admit one at a time. Then filling the cavity as well as they could with the stones and brushwood, struck a light and began to descend the damp, slippery steps cut in the old red sandstone, and soon found themselves far underneath the foundations of the old Castle.

'What's that?' sharply ejaculated the front man, as he convulsively grasped the arm of his companion.

'Nothing, you fool, but the splash of water,' and their voices seemed to roll like muffled thunder.

'I could have sworn I saw a face like that of the friar from whom I took this plan, but doubtless 'twas my fancy.'

And although now and then again the rush of some frightened rat or the peculiar sound of dropping water somewhat startled them, nothing occurred until after descending a further flight of steps they consulted the plan and felt they must be somewhere near the Cathedral.

'I don't quite like the situation, Phil,' said the youngest of the two.

'Oh, keep up your pluck. Think, what it will bring us if we are the discoverers of this much-talked of treasure.' This seemed to reassure them both. All unconscious of danger, at length, they came upon what seemed to be the end blocked, but turning round they observed three other subterranean ways, apparently leading in different directions. Passing into one of these, they had not explored long before they decided to go back, and under cover of night, get a larger stock of illuminants. But oh! little they thought that they, who had helped to hang and then plunder the

Monks, had themselves seen the light of Heaven for the last time. They had taken the wrong passage, and their lights were well nigh exhausted. They groped for two hours, till the last candle was nearly burned out. Twelve hours later they were far – far from the track by which they entered.

Their names were posted up for weeks as deserters from the Castle guards. But no tidings came. Troublous times immediately succeeded these events, when, on the death of Henry, the West was plunged into the fierce turmoil of rebellion, and the old city was once again besieged, and then by cruel persecution Mary restored the old faith and Elizabeth completed the work of her father.

Amid these scenes, the story of the hidden treasure became but a vague legend. The thoughts of men, were concentrated on issues of more immediate interest, but the story still survived, and when Cromwell's men stabled their horses in the stately pile traces still remained of vain searching whilst in later times little or no thought was given to what all deemed but an old myth, till the following story revived it with startling realism.

•

Eighteen years ago, when the restoration of Exeter Cathedral was in progress, Richard Horatio Snelgrove, Sir Gilbert Scott's representative, was sitting at breakfast in his apartments on Southernhay, when the maidservant entered and informed him that a 'man wished to speak with him'. Snelgrove, who was a pleasant, good-hearted, unceremonious person, said 'show him up.'

In a few seconds a short, thick-set,

sandy-haired individual stood before him. He was of the mason's labourer type, and the Architect, still going on with his meal, said pleasantly, 'Well, my man, and what's your business with me?'

'Well, sir,' he began, 'my name is Abraham Ganniclift and I live in Pancras Lane, I'm a jobbing mason.'

'And want a job,' joined in Mr Snelgrove.

'No, sir, thank'ee I've got plenty to do, but hearing that you was the gentleman that's doing up the Cathedral, and have been finding relics, I thought as this (holding up a small brown-paper parcel, about 8 inches by 4) might be interesting to you, but perhaps I'd better tell'ee all about it.'

'Certainly,' said Snelgrove, becoming rather interested, 'go on.'

'Well, eight years ago come this May,

me and my mate George Cox, as was killed repairing a tunnel on the South-Western, we were repairing the old sewer in High Street, just opposite Stephen's Bow, and George suddenly says, 'Well, I'm blowed if my pickaxe ain't gone slap through that crack,' pointing to a narrow hole in the bottom of the ground we were excavating. Well, we see it was a hole, so we set to work, cleared away some of the earth, and found there was a large opening beneath. So George drops a stone down and listens, and it made a hollow sound, and he distinctly heard a kind of ringing echo. And says George to me 'Abe,' says he, 'blest if there ain' a vault here.'

The hole was now big enough to put my head through. So we tied a candle to a bit of string and lowered it into the hole, and George held my legs whilst I thrust my head and shoulders in. There was a slight rush of cold air, which put the candle out. So I drew back and George got a small lantern, and I had another try. It looked precious dark at first, but in a little time my sight got clearer, and I could see we were above a passage but in the sandstone.

Just then our ganger, Sam Casely, he bawled out,'What's up down there?' So we told him, and he had a look, and we decided to make a bigger opening and explore further.'

Snelgrove had by this time become intensely interested, and all the more so as Ganniclift seemed in no hurry to reveal the contents of the paper parcel. So placing himself in a more comfortable position on his chair, he eyed the parcel and said 'Yes, go on.'

'Well, sir,' continued the mason, 'we

made an opening large enough for one to pass through. Casley got a ladder which touched the bottom about the tenth rung, and George, who was a daring sort of fellow (in fact it cost his life going in after his brother-in-law, whilst earth in that tunnel was still falling) – George he went first. He walked carefully along, speaking now and then, and his voice was like muffled thunder as he got further off. Presently he came up the ladder and said 'There's a lot of steps at the end of where I have been, which seem to lead to a still deeper place; it might be a water pit, and darned if I like going down alone, it's so awful deathy.'

So Casley says, 'Go with him, Abe.'

So with a couple of candles and the lantern, down we went. We felt cold air, and George, who was no fool, said there must be a opening somewhere. We went on about fifty yards, and then we commenced to descend the rather slippery steps which, as far as I could guess, were somewhere under the end of Martin's Lane, and where three other openings from three other directions seemed to lead to the one under the Green, in the direction of the Cathedral. I got a bit uneasy, and wanted to go back, but George, he said, 'Dash it, there's no fear, let's have a look through here,' pointing to the passage under the Green as we considered. We had not got many steps when George he shouted 'Stand back.'

I clutched his arm and saw him staring and holding the lantern at arm's length before him. 'Do you see that, Abe,' but it was misty, and I said 'No, what is it?'

'Why, them two skeletons squatting there.'

I began to see more clearly, and, sure enough, sir, there they were in what seemed to have been a sitting posture against a heap of earth which had evidently fallen in and blocked further progress that way. Well, this rather scared us, and we went back to report. But somehow we missed our way. We knew we had gone further than our hole could have been, and we found no steps, think how perplexing it was, and even George looked a bit scared.

But poor George he was always cool, and he says, 'Let us turn back as if we were coming up first', and from our first impressions we concluded which passage was ours, and we had not gone far when we found the steps, and heard the welcome voice of Casley bawling down that hole, as he was getting rather anxious about us.

We told him what we had seen, and he supplied us with buckets and an old box, and with Jim Brewster, who volunteered to go with us, we went again, and made straight for the skeletons to fetch 'em up. But bless your soul, sir, when George touched 'em they just rattled down together like a bundle of untied sticks. So we placed the bones in the buckets and box, and in two turns they were brought up with a few things mixed with the bones. There was quite a mob round it as they were placed in King's Alley, awaiting instructions for taking them to the Cemetery. Several gents, as calls themselves astronomers or something, said from the buckles and other things they were skeletons of soldiers killed perhaps in the early wars. But I did one thing, sir, which perhaps I shouldn't. In moving the bones I found besides one of them, this little metal box.'

And opening his parcel he showed the architect what he had up to this moment held so tantalising in his hand. Snelgrove rose from his chair to examine the articles, which consisted of a thin metal box, the hinges of which were rusted off. Inside was a quaint but very rusty key, and a small piece of discoloured parchment, upon which an unmistakeable ground plan of St Peter's was drawn, with four lines leading from opposite points to a spot indicated by a round dot at the right hand corner of the South Tower, and at the outer end of each line were the letters C, CK, K, W.

'But how do you account for your possession of this?' enquired the architect.

'Well, you see, sir,' said the mason, turning rather red, 'I thought it a curiosity, and as whoever it belongs to had no use for it, 'George he says to me, 'You keep it and if its worth anything, we'll share it.'

Snelgrove smiled, and remarked that they had been a long time finding anybody sufficiently interested. 'You see, sir, 'twas like this, we were afraid to say anything for a time and then poor George he got killed, and I really thought no more of it until this restoration business came up, and then it struck me that perhaps you'd like to have it, and if its worth anything I should give George's widow part of it, as the things are no use to us.'

A long train of thought was passing through the Architect's brain as the man had been speaking, for during his superintendence of the work at the Cathedral he had become acquainted with many of the stories and traditions of the edifice. 'And what about the passages, did you explore further?'

'Oh yes, but we hadn't much time, as ours was a contract job; but we managed to go a long way up each passage, but found that they had fallen in and were so rotten, that it was dangerous to proceed, and the one under the Cathedral Yard was quite blocked up, for we tried to see if we could clear it and found heavy masonry beyond.'

'Well,' said Snelgrove, 'suppose I give you a couple of guineas for them – will that satisfy you?'

'Most certainly,' said the mason, highly pleased.

The architect paid the money, and when the man had departed he thought of the old stories, still believed in by old vergers, of the Hidden Treasures. And on going to the Cathedral that morning he seemed to be more than usually absorbed in the structural condition of the South Tower. The seemingly heavy and somewhat unnecessarily massive masonry surrounding a certain tomb at the spot on the plan indicated strongly impressed him. So much so, that without mentioning his adventure to anybody else, he sent a detailed account to his chief, Sir Gilbert Scott, who was himself so interested in the matter as to come down to Exeter, and, after more fully acquainting himself with the particulars and peculiar position of a certain structure, thought the matter of sufficient importance to consult Dean Boyd. But that good but bigoted dignitary would not hear of so sacrilegious an excavation amongst the tombs being entered upon, and he begged that neither the architect nor his representative would speak or move further in the matter.

And so the mystery, which has been unsolved for over three hundred years, still remains, and the treasure which in these days would be worth over a million of money still is undiscovered; and, perhaps, will so remain until the classic pile crumbles into dust, or some unforeseen event renders it more possible and less sacrilegious to excavate amongst the tombs of old St Peter for the HIDDEN TREASURES lying beneath that sacred pile.

Through the North Gate:
A Story of
Christmas Eve

Partly from the diary of
Gregory Huntsdean,
Malster of this city, *Anno Domini* 17-

IRIS

1897

July - 'The barley Farmer Wheatear hath last sent in, not up to sample' - tut – tut – that's not it.

'Paid to Nicholas Greave in the Close' Nay! Nay! Wrong again.

August – September, First, second, third, aye! Here it is. The first mention in the diary of Cicely Aylmer:

'September 3rd 'Supped this eve at his house in the High Street with Master Peter Aylmer, the mercer. His daughter Cicely, who hath just left school, sat with us. A winsome maid, verily and hath a pleasant manner.'

Then again in December - 'Mistress Cicely is a model housekeeper. The mercer' house gets to look more home-like, more as if lived in. There are feminine nick nacks about the rooms (in the way, truly, yet still pleasant to look upon, which a man's eyes are unused to such trifles), that never were when Dame Renwick, Master Aylmer's worthy housekeeper, was sole mistress.

December 15th Went to see the mercer concerning the cotton business. He was out, so the trim waiting-maid showed me into the parlour behind the shop, and I had pleasant converse with Mistress Cicely. She looks moped. Saith old Exon is terribly dull. She shall have migraines and vapours soon.

'But,' said I, 'sure school could scarce have been lively.'

'Nay!' she answered, 'But there I had girl friends to talk to. While here's – there is none but Dame Renwick.'

'Thy father should seek friends for thee', said I. 'The young folk about here have their gaities. This very eve Musgrave, the chandler hath all his windows ablaze with lights, and I heard merry voices and much music as I passed. And on twelfth night there will be rare revels at the house of Master Guthram for one I know. Why sure Mistress Cicely, they will bid thee to that.'

'They have bidden me, I think,' she said indifferent, 'But father saith he cares not for such things. I may not go alone, and he will not permit me to be under obligation to any of his acquaintances.' And she leaned forward in her high-back chair, and tipped the little slippered foot thrust forth to the blaze, impatiently with her fan.

I am not a man to speak without dire deliberation, so there was silence for a few minutes, then –

'Thy father and I are old friends, Cicely, and Master Guthram's but a few door's off,' I said. 'If I told thy father that I go to the revels, and came here for thee, promising to bring thee home in good time, would he permit thee to go?'

She roused at once, and I felt repaid for the offer of the sacrifice so unwonted a dissipation will involve, when her eyes flashed up to me in the firelight and the pretty colour crept up over her neck and chin.

'Would you, indeed? Oh, father would allow me to go with thee, if thou asked him; he thinks so highly of thee. But! No!'

with a sigh, 'Tis a shame to take advantage of thy kindness to bore thee so. Thou canst not care for it any more than he does'.

'Nay!' said I, speaking an untruth valiantly, and suppressing my mortification at the ready fashion in which she accredited her father and me with similarity of tactics and feelings, when there are for certain nigh a score of years between our ages. 'I meant to go from the first; therefore 'twill put me about not at all. So! That is settled, provided thy father doth consent, and hither he comes in good time to be asked.'

Peter Aylmer hath given his consent readily. It may be that the fact that I have two ships successfully trading betwixt here and the West Indies, and am accounted a rich man beside, had somewhat to do with his graciousness!

January 7th - 'Went to the Guthram's last eve, and called in at Peter Aylmer's, according to promise. Mistress Cicely, very fair and winsome in some soft, flowered stuff, bids fair to be the reigning toast. The revels pass off well. There was one Godfrey Lestrange present, a stranger to Exon, biding in the neighbourhood with some friends. A malapert boy, I thought him, but Cicely, coming home, said he danced indifferent well, and that his step suited hers. I suppose that was why they stood up so often to face each other, though, surely, 'twere scarce necessary to nearly always sit down together too.'

March 10th - 'Peter Alymer brought his daughter Cicely to my house this afternoon to inspect the new picture I received from London by the coach last week. Verily, it seemeth as if a sunbeam had fitted into these dark old rooms, and Alack! out again.'

July -'Met Mistress Cicely in the High Street by St Stephen's Church this day. She had been shopping; her hands were full of packages, so 'twas perhaps but natural that Godrey Lestrange, who is again in Exeter, having met her just before they met me, should relieve her of some. 'twill be a boon when the young man's commission, for which he saith he is waiting, shall arrive.'

September 16th - 'My ship, the *Queen Anne*, just come into port. Hath made a very prosperous voyage. Verily, Mistress Gregory Huntsdean could flaunt in silken braveries with the best.'

September 17th - 'Went to the mercer's to acquaint Master Aylmer of my success this eve. He sounded me concerning shares in the *Queen Anne*, or any other venture, *For thou art ever in luck*, he said.'

'Aye!' said I, 'But that were too much to ask of a mere acquaintance –a friend. Now were we of kin?' –

'Of kin!' he said, and sighed, 'But that's impossible.'

'Not impossible, There is Cicely –'

'Cicely! A child and thou –'

'Old enough to be her – elder brother, thou woulds't say. But Cicely is eighteen and I – Well, tis but May and September at the worst. Not May and December, and even such matters as that *have* been happy. I can give her gew-gaws and fripperies enough to turn every other citizen's wife green with envy, and what do women want more? Whereas this penniless soldier. This Lestrange –'

'Why does thou harp so upon Lestrange? Soleath! I tell thee, man, he never cometh hither. I have actually never set eyes upon Lestrange, so tis little he can be in Cicely's company. Moreover, she knows my will too well to have anyting to say to a frog-eating Frenchman, as I understand this fellow is on the father's side.'

November – 'My second ship hath come into port. Master Aylmer, who hath received high honor, in so much as he hath been elected Mayor of this our ancient City, hath shares in her for the voyage on which she starts next week. Mistress Cicely hath promised to become my wife. When a man hath his two score years and ten behind him, there is little time left him for waiting, so the marriage is to take place on Christmas Day.'

December 23rd - 'Cicely hath made me promise to leave her in peace tomorrow. She hath much to do in the old home ere she quits it for good, she saith, so this eve I bade her farewell till Christmas morning. She is very shy, and full of maidenly reserve, my fair little sweetheart. This eve I came as near a caress as she hath ever allowed. Methought I might venture to take one kiss, but she twisted away her cheek, and held out her hand, so I was fair to content myself with laying my lips to the dainty fingers, whereon my ring gleams bright.'

'Thinking of Cicely, and of my near approaching marriage, I was opposite Martin's Lane before I discovered that I had left the stick, that an ague doth occasionally seize me in the knee renders a necessary companion, at the Mayor's house. This, that I carried this evening, happening to be my favourite staff of ebony, with silver-gilt head, I re-traced my steps.'

'There were lights in some of the windows of Bedford House as I passed, and some unseemly noises issuing there from, so I paused awhile to listen, but as they presently ceased, went on again. Tis pity, indeed, to see so noble a mansion let out thus in tenements to the poorer sort. I hear that there is talk of pulling it down, and erecting a terrace of decent houses on the site, which I pray soon be done.'

'Master Aylmer's door was not yet barred for the night, so I entered quietly, intending to possess myself of the stick, which I had left in the passage, and come away again, without disturbing anyone; but there were two or three canes together, and by the time, jumbling quietly in the darkness, I had discovered which was mine, the sound of voices in the parlour, whose door was open, letting a narrow patch of light stream out into the further end of the long passage, had arrested my attention. One was Cicely's, and curious to know to whom she was talking, for I knew her father was out, and Dame Renwick had retired just as I left. I stepped forward, keeping carefully in the shadow.

She was standing in the middle of the room and holding her hand, which he was rubbing vigorously with a kerchief, as if the ivory skin stood in need of polishing, was – of all persons, the man who Cicely's father thinks hath never crossed his threshold – Godfrey Lestrange.

'And, hey! for the son of Vulcan!' he was saying, as I came within earshot, and then they both laughed.

He was evidently just going, so I did not make my presence known, but slipping out quietly, loitered near the door till I had seen him come out and go up the street, when I went home. But, my present forbearance notwithstanding, thou will have to understand, Mistress Cicely, that there must be no sons of Vulcan, nor sons of d----d Frenchmen, nor anybody else's sons, loitering round Mistress Huntsdean after the morrow's morrow.

On the morrow, being Christmas Eve, we are bidden, Master Aylmer and I, and about a dozen of her prominent citizens – to dine late with Master Gardiner in the Close and sample a rare vintage of Spanish port he hath just received. And as Mistress Cicely hath forbidden me the Mercer's house, I shall go.

December 24th – We left Master Gardiner's just before 9 of the clock, being wishful to pass the gates before the porters closed them. On the further side of the Broadgate, we three – Master Jennifer, the Mayor and I – who had started together, and had been walking linked arm-in-arm for mutual support, for Master Gardiner's port is of the strongest, should have parted company; Master Alymer's way lying up the street; mine, for a little space, in the same direction; and Master Jennifer's house being by the North Gate. But, we having withdrawn our support from Master Jennifer, he, without ado, sank down in a shifting posture against the wall, and told us, with tipsy gravity, he intended staying there, as the earth was playing strange pranks, the ground, so he said, rising up and the house bending down to meet it.

So we twain, thinking it not seemly that a bailiff of the city should be found in that condition by the watch, got Master Jennifer upon his feet, took him by the arms again, and went down the High Street, resolute to see him safe to his own door.

'Ho! Old Peter?' said the mayor who, when in his cups, is ever given to moralising – as we drew near the Carfaix that stands at the four ways; though the townsfolk grew impatient and ask how much longer it is to block the streets, seeing there is greatly increasing traffic at this juncture.

'Ho! Old Peter!' to the image on the side of the conduit, 'still at thy post?'

Master Jennifer burst into a loud guffaw. 'That old Peter!' he cried, 'Why Peter hath ever looked towards the river. He is on the other side the conduit, man'.

'If you's not old Peter, he's not on the Carfoix at all,' said the Mayor; which is indeed the fact, as they would well have known had they been sober. Yet now nothing would content them, but they must go round to t'other side to see; and being not a whit more satisfied then, back we all came again to the Eastern side, then round again till, having circled the Carfaix a time or two more, why, of a truth, what with the wine we had drunk, and the darkness, the moon having gone behind a cloud, and the streets being but poorly lighted, we knew not, when we started to leave the conduit, and the dispute still unsettled, whether our faces turned North or South.

However, we should soon find out our whereabouts, said the Mayor, and so proved, for having taken but a few steps, Master Aylmer, who was walking on the outside, slipped on something on the roadway, and but barely saved himself from falling and dragging us down with him.

'Marry!' he cried, as we stood still all three. 'Now know I where we are. This is none other than South Gate Street and this the Butcher's Row. The reek of the shambles is in my nostrils, and 'twas the refuse in the kennel that caused me slip but now. Right about face, my friends! Right about face and keep straight on.'

And we did right about face, and keep straight on, watching our feet warily all three; and save for the trifling mishap that, with eyes upon the ground, we did not see the Carfoix, looming large before us, till we were close upon it, and so met it first with our heads, which misadventure went near to upsetting our equilibrium again, we got safe to the North Gate, and the porch of Master Jennifer's house, where I left my worthy fellow citizens, and hastened home, for Dame Quantly hath a rare tongue to scold when a man overstays his time.'

Here the diary abruptly ceases, therefore the veracious chronicle of these events must even finish the stay in his own words, and to do so must crave indulgence of his readers, while he harketh back to the evening of Christmas Eve's eve, and the interview betwixt Godfrey Lestrange and Cicely Aylmer, which old Gregory Huntsdean had come in upon when he returned for his cane, as his diary tells.

Scarcely, on that evening, has he, the elderly suitor, passed the threshold of his betrothed's house, when Cicely, who had accompanied him to the door, is joined by her young lover, Godfrey Lestrange who had stepped out from the friendly shadow of an adjoining porch.

'Oh, Godfrey! This is rash,' Cicely cries, drawing him hastily into the passage. 'He may look back at any minute. Thou wilt have to come into the parlour'.

'I did but come to tell thee that all goes well, dear love,' he whispers eagerly.

The carriage is to await us at a lone farm house, a mile out on the North Road, whether we shall ride, thou on a pillion behind me, for a coach or two riding horses would attract attention in the streets so late, whereas riding pillion the watch will but think us belated country folk.'

'But it is terrible to have to leave one's home thus, and so slyly, Godfrey. I would there were any other way.'

'But there is none, dear heart. And for the slyness of the proceedings, think not of that, think that if I had not chanced to return to Exon a week since, on the morrow's morrow thou wouldst'.

'Oh Godfrey! Hush!' she interrupts, 'I shudder at the thought. And as thou hast said, twere useless to plead with my father. He will not even hear me indeed when I have tried, but ever saith that being an honourable maiden, having promised of my own free will –'

'But thou didst not promise of thy own free will.'

'Aye! But I did. There's the rub. They, father and Dame Renwick, had been urging me so. Thou wert away, and then Agnes Gunthrum told me that thou were troth-plight to thy kinswoman in France, and when I thought that thou hadst been but mocking me -. And they took good care to give me no time to change my mind. Such haste is not seemly, is it, Godfrey? To be betrothed but in November, and married at Christmas. Was ever maid in such a woeful case?'

'Yes, to be married in the merry Christmas time, truly, but not to Gregory Huntsdean, dear heart. Courage sweet love –'

'Hark!' interrupts Cicely, as a sound of

movement becomes audible, 'Surely that is Dame Renwick! Thou must go at once Godfrey. Am I not unmaidenly to dismiss two lovers thus within ten minutes.'

'Faith! Twas time to dismiss the other,' she adds, as she takes up a candle to light this lover out. 'For tonight, when he went, he kissed me.'

'He kissed thee? And thou, Cicely –'

'My hand! Only my hand, not my lips!,' she says, laughing, and holding out the little hand that had been so desecrated.

Godfrey takes it in his, and proceeds vigorously to rub away the kiss.

'Courage love!' he says again. 'There is only tomorrow to win through, and then: Hey! for the Son of Vulcan.'

•

At half-past nine on Christmas Eve Godfrey Lestrange is standing in the shadow of the porch of Master Aylmer's house. A few minutes later the casement window above opens gently, and something flutters softly to the ground. It is the signal agreed upon. Godfrey steps out for an instant into the moonlight, picks up the kerchief and puts it in his breast. A very few seconds more and the high, narrow door is opened quietly, wrapped in a thick riding cloak, that entirely conceals the contour of her slim form, and with her sunny curls and nearly the whole of her face, too, buried in a huge quilted satin-lined hood, edged with fur, is in his arms.

'I thought Dame Renwick never would go to bed,' she says, as soon as her lips are free for speech. 'Even now we must make haste to be out of sight, for fear she should come downstairs again.'

So down the street they hurry,

keeping close to the houses, and go somewhat in the shadow of the over-hanging upper stories, getting safe to the Carfoix without encountering a single soul, for 'tis too late for ordinary passengers, and too early yet for mummers and the waits who will by-and-bye announce the glad tidings of Christmas along the highways and bye-ways of the City.

'This seems like driving it very close,' Godfrey says as they hasten along, 'to leave our flight till the very eve before the wedding; yet we are greatly gainers by the delay, for on the morrow, no one will expect the bride to be stirring early, so thou wilt not be missed till daylight, which will give us a ten hours' start, and even when they do discover our flight, the stablemen will be heavy after their Christmas carouse, so more time will be wasted, till, ere they get horses to follow us, we shall be far on our way to Gretna Green.'

To all which Cicely assents.

A few paces down North Gate Street they pause at open doors of an inn yard, whence, in answer to Godfrey's low whistle, a stableman emerges, leading a heavy-built horse, furnished with a saddle and pillion.

'I will not mount till we have passed through the gate, dear heart.' Godfrey says, as he lifts his lady love into the pillion and takes the bridle from the man.

As they come in sight of the North Gate Cicely utters an exclamation of dismay.

'Oh Godfrey! The Gate! Tis shut!'

'Of course, love. Tis past nine of the clock. But a golden key will unlock it in a twinkling,' he adds reassuringly.

Yet, for all his brave words, Godfrey's heart misgiven him as he notices that the porter's house is in darkness.

'Now a plague upon him,' he cries again, this time not under his breath, when his second and third knocks have remained unanswered. 'They must sleep sound, unless, which the saints forbid, he hath gone out.'

He is raising his whip for a fourth knock, a knock which shall bring down the house, or an answer, which would be more to the purpose, when the window over the door is pushed violently open, and a night-capped head thrust forth.

'Who's there? And what do you want?' a surly voice demands.

'To pass through your gate, Master Porter,' Godfrey answers. 'We be two country folk who have been in the city all day and have over-stayed our time for returning.'

'Then you'll even have to stay till morning,' snaps the porter. 'I be gone to bed, and I'll not unbar my gate against this night.'

'But, Master Porter!' cries Godfrey, repressing a less courteous appellation with difficulty, 'We must –'

'Must? Hoity! Toity! Who be ye to order an officer of the city? Must, indeed! Then I tell thee I must not open my gate till morning. And I will not, to any less a personage, that is, than the Mayor, the head of our city,' and so having settled the matter, was drawing to the casement, when the door of Master Jennifer's house opposite opens, and out into the street, his eyes blinking in the moonlight, and his gait a trifle more unsteady than when he entered the house, comes the Mayor.

Now, 'desperate ills require desperate remedies,' and a desperate idea, a forlorn hope, occurs to the mind of Godfrey Lestrange.

Drawing courage from remembrance of the fact that Master Aylmer, even if sober, could not know him, they having never chanced to meet, and trusting that, being evidently deep in his cups, he may even be prevented from recognising Cicely, the young man steps boldly forward, and stops him.

'Master Mayor!' he cries, and speaking hastily, for every moment is precious, and the porter, seeing who has come upon the scene, pushed the window open again, and leans out. 'Master Mayor! We be country folk who have tarried so late at a friend's merrymaking in the city, that we find the gate's closed for the night, and the porter were, who is a surly rogue, doth refuse to open. Or rather, he saith he will open, to no less a personage than your worship. Now, tis imperative that we get home tonight. Therefore, I make bold to ask your worship –'

'But! Marry! I know not who you are. I may be conniving at some misdoing, and, any gait, why shall I put myself about?'

'Because this damsel is in great distress at the porter's churlishness, and we have ever heard that Master Aylmer is ever gallant to the sex, and that no female in distress doth appeal to him in vain!'

'Now, marry!' cries the Mayor. 'That is truth. So since the porter will have it no other way, I will even lead the horse through. So throw open your gate, Master Porter!' to the porter, who has by this time appeared upon the scene, so wholly dressed as to belie his declaration that he had been abed.

Cicely, having heard the result of the colloquy, draws her hood closer over her face, and buries her little pointed chin deeper in her furs, and, for the rest, trusts to the distance the good horse's sturdy height places between her face and the Mayor's eyes, and, much more, to the influence of Master Gardiner's port, and what Master Aylmer has since imbibed at Master Jennifer's. And her trust is not misplaced. Indeed the Mayor has enough for his eyes to do in watching his feet, and once beyond the gate Godfrey, on the other side of the horse, connives to stay him in the deepest shade.

As Master Aylmer releases the bridle, 'We thank thee right heartily, Master Mayor!' Godfrey says, and placing his foot in the stirrup, prepares to mount.

But they are not to get off yet.

'Thy hand, lady, thy hand to kiss,'

cries the Mayor, detaining Cicely with a hand upon her horse's shoulder. 'Nay, be not shy! Many a gallant would ask a kiss from the lips for such a service.'

But it is not from shyness Cicely hesitates. The very spirit of mischief appears to have entered into her, for, drawing off her heavy riding gloves, she manages deftly to loosen a ring, she always wears upon the middle finger from its accustomed place close to the knuckle, and, holding it dexterously suspended on the tip of the finger, contrives to drop it into Master Aylmer's palm as he bends over her hand.

Now, the ring has been so evidently shaken into his hand that the Mayor cannot think it an accident; it has been done so secretly, too, that he can but receive it in silence, and so he stands still in the doorway with his hat in his hand, bowing as low as is compatible with the preservation of his equilibrium, while the now doubly weighted horse jogs warily down the steep declivity, and then, re-entering the city, makes the best of his way homewards, dropping the trinket, as he goes, into an inner pocket for future examination, and straightway forgetting all about it.

•

The Mayor's household is early astir on Christmas morning, Dame Renwick scolding and bustling about energetically.

Daylight, creeping through the chinks of the shutters, has just begun to make the candles look sickly and faint, when one of the maids remarks to Mistress Renwick that Mistress Cicely lies late.

'Tis time she was awakened,' says Dame Renwick, and begins, with much panting – for she is a roundabout old body, to mount the narrow, twisting stairs.

A knock at Cicely's door receiving no answer, she opens it quietly and steps in.

Another minute, and, with face as white as her apron, she has traversed the long passages between the two rooms and is beating frantically with her fists on the panels of the Mayor's door.

'Master! Master Aylmer!' she cries, breathlessly, 'In Heaven's dear name! Get up! Cicely's bed hath not been slept in, and her riding cloak and hood are gone from the back of her door, where I saw them but yester eve.'

Thus hurriedly roused – perchance from dreams of the marvels of money-making he and his son-in-law-elect will accomplish in the future, Peter Aylmer, in hot haste, begins to throw on the garments he had put off the night before.

As he lifts the coat something falls from an inner pocket, and, rolling to the leg of the bed, lies there glistening in the dawn light.

It is Cicely's ring.

The Mayor picks it up and holds it out in his broad palm, staring hard at it, and trying to recall where he has seen it before.

Suddenly he sits down heavily on the side of the bed, and stares still harder, while his jaw drops, and the rich ripe colour fades from his cheeks.

Like a flash the truth has burst on him.

MISS JEFFERSON'S BABY
A STORY OF CHRISTMAS EVE, 1781

FREDERICK THOMAS
1881

Why does my lady of Rougemont do,
On this terrible night, through the drifting
  snow,
To kneel at a humble grave in prayer,
Leaving a wreath of immortelles there?
Ah! why, indeed! For the night is chill,
And the snow-storm sweeps o'er David's Hill,
Piling the flakes on the tombstones high,
That the moon, as she fitfully peeps from
  the sky,
Seems to fill every part of that sacred ground
As with white-winged angels watching around.

But for years, e'er time had tinged her hair,
Each Christmas Eve had she been there;
And, sure as came round each Christmas Day,
The worshippers looked as they passed that
  way,
For they knew a fresh wreath would be
  found, instead
Of the one that had crumbled, all withered
  and dead.
Come, Father James, we pray you tell
The story they say you know so well.

'Tis fifty years this very night,
The air was cold, and the roads as white,
The 'yule logs' crackled, and sent their glow
Through the casements bright to the
  dancing snow.
The welcome sounds of the Christmas waits
Were heard beyond the City gates
I remember it well, though I was but a boy,
For I always looked forward with youthful joy

To Christmas-tide, when I dared to show
I knew the use of the mistletoe.
Real Christmas weather as used to be,
And a frost as now we but seldom see;
Though they'd not believe 'twas Christmas
  at all
Unless the waits had given a call.
And we waited the coming, with great delight,
Of Christmas Eve and New Year's night,
For Lord of the Manor, the Parson or Squire,
Were never forgot by St David's choir.
Two pounds apiece at least 'twas worth
Our singing 'Good Will and Peace on Earth',
Although at times, I am sorry to say,
It didn't wind up in a peaceful way.

But I'll tell my story. We always met
At Jefferson's cottage, and 'Jeff' would get
A jug of 'flipp', sweet, strong, and warm,
Which was proof, as he said, against frost
  or storm

'Jeff' was clerk of the parish. His wife was dead;
But she'd left him a treasure as dear in her stead,
Their only child, his darling Grace,
With her mother's love and her mother's face;
And the gloom which tell with the loss of
  his wife
Was dispelled by this heaven-sent light of
  his life;
For Grace was loving as she was fair,
With her deep blue eyes and flaxen hair,
And, though twenty summers she'd
  scarcely seen,
More than one smitten swain at her feet had been,
Or to ask the old man if he thought she
  would smile
On their suit, but he answered them all
  'Wait awhile.'

We'd finish the 'flip', and prepared to start,
But the wind howled so fiercely, we'd scarcely the
heart;

And when Jefferson rose to open the door,
It rushed into the place with a terrible roar,
Filling the room with the flakes of snow, -
I began to despair we should ever go.
'Twas decided we should, but, as I
   was young,
And hadn't before with the choir sung,
'Twas settled that I should remain in
   the place,
And be company there for Mistress Grace.
We drew our chairs to the blazing logs,
Which sparkled and hissed on the
   'hangle dogs',
That gave to our fancy such fantastic shapes,
Now castles, now cities, now angels, now apes.
We were laughing to see stately palaces fall,
When we heard at the window old Jefferson
   call –
'Grace! Open the door, my child! Open I pray,
'Be quick, dear!' he cried, as she rushed
   to obey.

Then he placed in her arms what appeared,
   by the glow
Of the log, was a bundle all covered in snow.
Then he quitted the cottage, and Grace's eyes
Bespoke her amazement and surprise.
But, O, how great was her delight
When she beheld so strange a sight!
The bundle, opened, disclosed to Grace
A baby girl, with an angel face.
Like yesterday, I can see her there,
As she kissed the cherub with tenderest care,
And fed it, and warmed it, and hummed it
   a song,
And wondered to whom did the
   stranger belong
Then the fairy tales flitted across her
   young mind,
In her girlish desire some solution to find.
Had she found a real princess, by pixies
   preserved
From a terrible fate, which no baby deserved?

When the party returned, all were anxious
  to know
What old Jefferson had (as he told them)
  to show.
His story was short. 'I was waiting,' he said,
'For the rest of the choir, who had gone
  on ahead.
I could scarcely see for the blinding sleet,
When I fancied I heard a faint wail at
  my feet.
I had sheltered myself 'neath the Eastgate wall
From the pierceing wind and the heavy fall.
And I thought that I heard the faint
  wailing again,
But weakly, and helpless, and seeming in pain.
I kicked a large heap by my side, when, lo!
That bundle, you see there, lay buried in snow.
I was startled at first, but my only thought
Was to do at once what a Christian ought;
So Grace, for my darling, I give it to you
A sister, for just an hour or two;

And if nobody claims it, the parish must bear
The burden of this, so we'll send it there.'

Grace looked at her father, and begged she may
Keep the dear little thing over Christmas Day.
He gave his consent, but, ah! little he thought
With what danger that little concession
*   was fraught,*
For when two long days had flitted by,
The old man said, with a moistened eye,
'Come Grace, my daughter, the little waif
Must go where it's sure to be happy and safe.'
She begged so hard that another day
She might keep the babe, ere 'twas taken away.
But her father shook his head, and smiled,
Kissed her fair forehead, and said, 'My child,
To keep it with us would be unwise,
And may seem somewhat strange in other eyes.
The world is too prone to misconstrue,
And condemn what e'en angels dare to do.'
She pleaded hard, and the old man saw

That his case was lost, and her love was law.
They kept the babe, but, strange to say,
Suitors were scarcer from that day.

Fifteen Christmas Eves had flown,
And Eve to a beautiful girl had grown;
They called her Christmas Eve, you know,
Because of the night she was found in the snow.
Old 'Jeff' had gone from this world of strife
To join his good and loving wife;
And Grace her tears of sorrow had shed
Where the daisies grew o'er her parent's head.
But the 'bread on the waters' was surely cast,
When, in that night of storm and blast,
She took the foundling to her heart,
And kindled a love that should never depart.
Through a long weary sickness Eve nursed her
  with care
And at her side was ever there,
While o'er her 'mother' she gently bent
Like a guardian angel from Paradise sent;

For Eve was her solace by day and
  by night,
The flowers on her pathway, her life and her
light.

The proud lord Lord of Rewe had died,
And his heir had taken himself a bride;
There was joy at the Manor, the 'yule log'
  burned,
For the happy pair had just returned.
'Twas Christmas Eve, and the sky was clear,
And the song of carollers sounded near;
The air was fresh, and the moon
  shone bright,
Pouring its rays of liquid light.
So full and grand, that 'Heaven's gem'
Seemed to herald the Star of Bethlehem.
'My lord seems sad', the lady cried.
'This should not be at Christmastide.
What ails my love, I pray you to say.
Why thus with you, when all is gay?'

He drew her gently to his breast,
'Alas! Tis true, I have no rest;
And but for the love I know you feel,
My heart would fail me to reveal
At such a time, on such a night,
The cause of my sorrow, which seems to blight
My every joy, and bids me sigh
When mirth should reign and thou art nigh.
My sire was proud of the family tree,
And hugged our ancient pedigree;
And often he'd say, with his fiercest frown,
'Who dares to drag our pedigree down
By union with an inferior line,
Shall be no son or heir of mine.'
He looked upon me with jealous care,
For, were she virtuous and fair,
Twold weigh a nought, unless her line,
Was of ancient date as thine.

But O! my heart was young and warm,
I had no fear – I saw no harm,

If I should wed what pleased me,
E'en without wealth or pedigree,
I wooed and won a beauteous maid
Of humble birth, but was afraid
To tell my sire, whose wrath I feared
For sake of her to me endeared.
Too long he thought I'd been away,
Bid me return without delay.
My regiment, too, was like to be
Soon sent to face the enemy.
I brought her to the lovely West
I'd made resolve, and thought it best
Should I confess what I had done,
To plead excuse, through her I'd won.
I had arranged that she should dwell
In a pretty cot near Exwick dell;
And she was content to know that I,
Though oft away, was ever nigh.

But on our joy a shadow fell,
Which I battled bravely to dispel;

For the angel of death was hovering near,
Torturing me, mid hope and fear,
And our baby girl scarce saw the light
Ere the mother's spirit had taken flight.
The vow I made in that humble place,
As my tears fell on her dear dead face,
I have not kept, and my peace of mind –
Great Heaven! I fear I shall never find.
Look not with scorn, and you shall know
I never meant it should be so.

The child remained with the ancient pair,
Who never knew nor seemed to care.
Yet I was possessed of a foolish fear,
Lest my child, and my home should be too near;
For I had resolved, without delay,
To join my regiment for the fray.
I knew one Andre Fabian,
Who'd been my father's serving man,
Returning to the South of France,
And it occurred that he, perchance,

Might take the child, and that his wife
Would tend it well, and save his life;
For the child was weak, and should I send
To South of France, a double end
By its removal would be served –
Both child and secret would be preserved.

I thought my plan had been well laid,
And when a long adieu I bade
To home and friends, I little knew
To peace of mind I'd bid adieu.
He had arranged that they should leave
For Les Martignea on Christmas Eve,
In the trading vessel Fleur de Mai,
Which was to sail on Christmas Day.
I bade him come to the Eastern Gate
As the old Cathedral clock struck eight;
The snow and sleet beat in my face
As I met him at the appointed place.
He took the child, and from that day,
What came of it, I cannot say.

I troubled but little through that long time,
By duty kept in a foreign clime;
But when to Europe I returned
To see my child, my bosom yearned.
I sought De Fabian, but alas!
The place a ruin, and the grass
With weeds around the dwelling grown,
Long vacant, was too plainly shown.
All I could gather was, that he
Had ruined been, and crossed the sea.

A dame I saw, who said she knew
De Fabian well, and Madam too;
And to my grief did she declare,
She never saw an infant there.
For years I sought my child to trace
In fruitless search from place to place.
Just twenty weary years have flown,
And now to you, sweet wife, I own.
Each Christmas Eve my heart is led
To mourn her if alive or dead.

But hark! the Christmas waits I hear,
With them the past comes up too clear.
You now know why, when all is glad,
My heart is torn, and I am sad'.

The Christmas waits had sung and
   played,
And my lord of Rewe came out and
   bade
Them enter, and partake of cheer,
And around the ashen log draw near.
'A Merry Christmas I pledge to you,
And welcome everyone to Rewe!'
His lordship said, when a servant came
To say a beggar man, whose name
He couldn't pronounce, 'But the fellow says
He was known to my lord in former days.'
Bid him come in, that I may see,'
His Lordship said 'who he may be;
He's welcome be he known or not,
To such as we this night have got.'

The man had scarcely passed the door,
The goblet was dashed upon the floor;
His lordship staggers with a groan-
'Great God, De Fabian! And alone!'
He sprang at this throat like a panther wild,
'My child! Wretch, what have you done with
  my child!
You took my infant, you took my gold,
But I'd have given a hundred-fold,
If what I gave in that pitiless storm
Could have saved my innocent child from harm.'

Mon Dieu! mi lor, vot do you say!
Is this in earnest or in play?
I wait outside the Westgate wall
Till I freeze, but you never come at all.
I wait till wiz snow I was nearly blind,
And I left when I think that you alter
  your mind.'
'Did I not give the gold to you?'
'Mon Dieu! I never receive a sou;

I get no child, I get no gold,
But wait all night in the bitter cold.
I lose my all, and I tramp this way,
In hope for some help on Christmas Day;
But instead of receiving what I expeck,
I find you take me by the neck.'

The waits looked on in fear and dread,
But I had heard what De Fabian said;
And my thoughts, in a moment, seemed to go
To the baby Old Jefferson found in the snow.
'Pray loose your hold, my Lord, I pray,
For I desire a word to say.
Was it twenty years, and on Christmas Eve?
If so, my lord, then I believe
That I on this matter can throw some light,
For an infant was found in the snow
   that night.
Your lordship speaks of the Eastgate wall,
He speaks of the West, and in that fall,
Of snow your lordship made mistake,

And let some evil villain take
Your child and gold, then on the ground
Left the babe to perish, where 'twas found.'
Twas then I related what I knew,
And in less than an hour my lord of Rewe,
With myself for a guide, gently knocked at
  the door
Of Wynard's Home for the worthy poor.

There was joy at the Manor, the logs were
  piled,
And the bells rang out for the long lost child;
And ere another Christmas came,
The young heir of Rougemont rode out to claim
The beautiful Lady Eve as his bride.
But there was one who stood by her side
On that bridal morn, whose kiss of love
She prised all earthly things above —
Her foster Mother, who felt that morn
A joy in her soul, that was Heaven-born.
At Rougemont Castle, there's mirth tonight,

Sweet music sounds, and the log burns bright;
But my Lady Eve, she would not miss,
E'en on such a boisterous night as this,
To visit the old Churchyard, and place
On the grave of her foster mother Grace,
That beautiful wreath, which is always seen
Each Christmas Day, looking fresh and green.
But hark! St David's Choir I hear,
And the day of peace and love draws near.
I've told my story and now you know
Who knelt tonight in the blinding snow;
And I see that I need not tell you why
There's a love in her heart that can never die!

Also available from **The Mint Press**

Christmas in Devon (2001)
Victorian Ghost Stories
Victorian Stories of Romance
Victorian Stories 'Round a Dartmoor Hearth

Christmas in Devon   Todd Gray (2000)

The Devon Almanac   Todd Gray (2000)

The Concise Histories of Devon Series
Roman Devon   Malcolm Todd (2001)
The Vikings and Devon   Derek Gore (2001)
Elizabethan Devon   Todd Gray (2001)
Devon and the Civil War   Mark Stoyle (2001)

The Devon Engraved Series
Exeter Engraved: The Secular City (2000)
Exeter Engraved: The Cathedral, Churches, Chapels and Priories (2001)
Devon Country Houses and Gardens Engraved (2001)
Dartmoor Engraved (2001)

The Travellers' Tales Series
Exeter (2000)
East Devon (2000)
Cornwall (2000)